D1099497

Say Hello

to Peter Ian Green

- 'PIG' for short.

There are six PIG books so far. It's best to

read them in this order:

1. **PIG** and the **Talking Poo**
2. **PIG** and the **Fancy Pants**
3. **PIG** and the **Long Fart**
4. **PIG** plays **Cupid**
5. **PIG** gets the **Black Death** (nearly)
6. **PIG** **Saves** the **Day**

PIG Saves the Day
by Barbara Catchpole
Illustrated by metaphrog

Published by Ransom Publishing Ltd.
Unit 7, Brocklands Farm, West Meon, Hampshire
GU32 1JN, UK
www.ransom.co.uk

ISBN   978 184167 618 0
First published in 2012
Reprinted 2013, 2014, 2015 (twice)

PIG

Saves the Day

Barbara Catchpole

Illustrated by metaphrog

Ransom

Don't worry!

Hi there! It's me! Pig! Is everything OK with you? Family alright? This is my last story for a bit. Gone quickly, hasn't it?

I'll really miss you. Not in a soppy way - in a manly way, of course.

Now this one starts a bit unhappily, but I don't want you to worry. No point you getting all upset. I know what you're like! It ends fine, really great. So hang in there!

The story is all about football. So if you don't like football but you like rugby or cricket instead, stop being so posh! (Just joking. I like rugby. It's all mud and wrestling. What's not to like?)

I can't see the point of cricket though.

Three arguments

Monday was a weird day. I had three rows in the same day. I never argue with people. I'm a bit of a wimp. I like people to be happy.

But that Monday I had three rows, one after the other. I'll tell you just like it happened. Perhaps you'll have a better idea about what went wrong. I haven't a clue.

Argument number one: Suki

08.00 in the Kitchen. Suki is gunking up her eyes.

Suki is my big sister. She IS big as well. She's nearly six foot, like my dad. Look, I had to turn her sideways to fit her in:

Suki's going out with a bloke who's really short. I mean, he can't even see her face without a ladder. She looks like Big Bird next to him. I found out his name was Kim.

(I hope she's not gunking up her eyes just for Kim. He doesn't carry a ladder EVERYWHERE with him, so he never actually gets to see her face – except from a long way away. I REALLY don't understand girls.)

Anyway.

Me:

'Kim – that's a girl's name, that is.'

Suki:

'No it's not, it's both.'

Me (in a silly sing-song voice, dancing about like a looney, wiggling my bottom):

'Girly name! Girly name! Girly name!'

Suki stopped putting gunk on her eyes. She got very red and started to shout:

'It's not! It's not! He's lovely! At least he isn't stupid like you! He doesn't try to have a girl's injection!* You can just shut up! I hate you! You're so IM-MAT-URE!'

* A footnote (we're doing footnotes now in English). For those of you who don't keep up with the trials of Pig, that's when I nearly died from the Black Death.

Wooahh! What was all that about? I'm her little brother. I'm supposed to tease her. It's my job.

Argument number two: Mum

08.15 in the kitchen. Mum is drinking tea. I am getting into my school stuff.

Harry the hamster was back in his cage. Mum had left it open on the floor. He'd just walked into it and she'd closed the door.

Harry's not happy though. He wants to break out again now. He spends his time trying to bite through the bars with his huge hamster teeth. He looks like Dean Gosnall.

I said:

    'Mum – why can't Harry wander about? At

    least he's happy then! Look at him now.

    He's like the Hamster in the Iron Mask!'

She said:

    'Because yesterday Gran nearly buttered

    him instead of her toast.

'Because Vampire Baby nearly sat down on him.*

'Because he leaves little poos everywhere.

'Because he probably leaves little wees, too, but they dry up. I think that was why your trainer was damp yesterday.

---

* Another footnote. (That makes two! My English teacher will be SO pleased.) I forgot that I was going to tell you our name for my baby brother. It's Vampire Baby. Mum calls him that because he sleeps all day and is awake all night. Or did I tell you that already?

'Because Suki will spike him with one of her

heels and he'll be Hamster Kebab.'

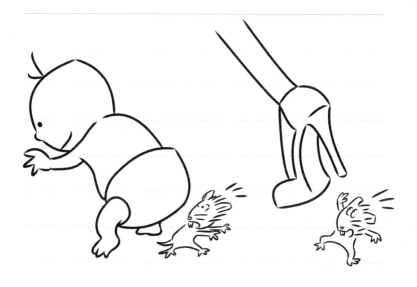

I asked:

'Why did he go back in his cage, Mum?'

'Because men don't know what they want,

Pig, and Harry is a male.

'Men say they know what they want. They say they want a nice clean cage with good food and a warm bed. They want lots of that cotton wool bedding stuff, I mean.

Then, I'm afraid that once they have it, they want 'out' again. I don't know if some men ever settle down, Pig.'

I said:

'Let him go – at least then he'll be happy.'

That was when she got upset.

> 'What about the rest of us, Pig? What
> about you? Life just isn't like that! We
> can't all have what we want and just
> wander about having fun.'

I don't get it. Why did she get so upset about a
hamster? Do YOU know what I said?

Or maybe it was about more than hamsters.

Argument number three: Dean Gosnall

Ten hundred hours on the school field. The bit
near the garden of the sad old bloke with
trousers up to his chin who shouts at us when
the ball goes over and who won't give it back.

15

I was in goal for our Year because Gary Blake
had dropped a frozen chicken on his foot. Now,
I like football, but I was a bit out of it
because nobody I lived with was talking to me
properly. I was upset.

I let the first goal in because I was watching
Tiffany play hockey.

The second goal – there were two crane flies
doing it on the goalpost. Actually doing it.

The third goal was a penalty and I dived the
wrong way.

The fourth goal I had an itchy bum and the
fifth I was trying to remember all the actors
in 'Doctor Who' because
I was bored. I couldn't
remember the name of
his last assistant and it
put me off.

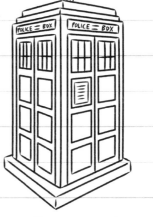

I saved the sixth one because I was waving at
Raj who was playing on the next field and I hit

it out with my waving hand. I'm sure it must have looked good.

I sort of lost interest after that because we stood no chance. But we only lost twelve – nil. I know we were only playing the year below us, but some of those kids are really big.

Dean Gosnall went mental at me:

'You loser, Pig! What's the matter with you? See this round thing? We call it a ball. Baaaaaaalllllllllllllllll! You're supposed to keep it out of the goal. That's the thing with the white posts, behind you! It's in the rules! You are a TOTAL DIVVY!

'You're not being goalie for my team EVER
AGAIN.'

Dean has more teeth than he has mouth, so he
was actually SPITTING at me. He looked like
Harry the Escaping Hamster.

Dean's friends came and stood behind him. Raj
came and stood beside me. Dean and I started

to push each other a little bit. You know, like you don't want to fight but you want to look big in front of your friends.

Then Sir broke it all up ('Calm down, calm down. What's this all about, ladies?') and sent us back to change.

Sir said:

    'You WERE rubbish, Pig. I'm dropping you

    from the match on Friday.'

Miss Goli

I was sitting on the steps by the art rooms and I was sad. It was all too much. I wasn't crying though – it was a windy day and something got in my eye.

Miss Goli was on duty. She's young and she's nice. She is new and she talks to you properly, like a real person. She only had to say:

　　'Whassup, Pig?'

and I was telling her all about the rows and the football match.

　　'Oh, you poor Pig!'
she said – and she sat down beside me and gave

me a tissue for the bit of dirt in my eye.

'Sometimes, you know, when people get
upset, it's because of something in THEM,
not something in YOU. Ask Sir again about
the football, I'm sure he'll say 'Yes'.'

Her name is 'Goli'! It was a sign! So I asked him again.

Please, Sir!

'... So Mr Strange, Sir, please let me play. I promise I'll do well. Please, Sir!'

'No.'

'It was just today.'

'No.'

'I didn't feel well.'

'No.'

'I was off my game.'

'No.'

'Are you still going out with Miss Hardcastle, Sir? You know I was in the stockroom ... '

'Yes, I am seeing the lovely Miss Hardcastle. Are you trying to blackmail me, Peter Ian Green? GREENmail me? You can if you like, but it won't help you and you're better than that.'

Now I felt mean.

'No Sir, I wouldn't do that! But will you please take me?'

'Um ... Let me think ... No.'

The curse of the pits

As it happened, though, Mr Strange had to take me.

Monday: Gary Blake fell over his crutches and broke his other leg. I got into trouble for laughing at registration.

Tuesday: The Zwing twins (Zwing One and Zwing Two) got chickenpox.

Wednesday: Sky Taylor's mum is a hippy and he said that after school on Friday he'd have to go to something to do with the full moon and trees. Wayne Baggott wanted to play, but he's more rubbish than I am.

Thursday: Frankie's mum was having twins and he had to stay at home to help his dad with the triplets and the puppy. (His dad's a bit careless.)

When she heard about it, Mum said:

> 'There's always somebody worse off, isn't there? He's REALLY careless!'

She sort of said it to herself and laughed her loud laugh quietly, because she wasn't talking to me.

Friday: Ryan Robbins was grounded because he'd lost his mum's car keys down a drain.

Raj had to travel to a huge family wedding in Birmingham ('Oh, Pig, please – my twelve aunts will be there. Hide me at your house.')

A bit of advice: never hide people at your house. It never ends well.

Also on Friday: Sir was in a foul mood because Sky's mum had boiled the footy shirts with his sister's pyjamas and now our kit was pink all over.

So Sir wasn't too pleased that he had to ask me to come to the match after all.

28

'You're on the bench, Pig. You can be a sub. You won't play.'

The Academy

We were playing the Academy. We wanted to win a lot because the Academy is SOOOOO perfect. Everything is new there. They have a big new glass building, more like a fish tank than a school. You can see into all the rooms from outside.

They all have new uniforms which they actually wear. There are more computers than children. There are more teachers than children. Everything looks like it's just come out of the car wash.

Even the changing rooms were lovely and warm,

with no black stuff on the walls. They had under-floor heating. I thought perhaps I'd try to get left behind and move in there. It was WAY nicer than our house.

So we had to win! It was a football thing.

Sir didn't even let me get changed:

'No point, Pig! You are not going to get a game. Stevie - get changed - you can be first sub. Jay, put that back - it's not yours! Yes, they will miss it.'

I was very disappointed. Our boys trotted onto the Academy's special all-weather pitch under floodlights. Our pink strip looked great next to their black-and-gold with the school crest on their pockets (NOT).

They had cheerleaders, too! No, no joke – cheerleaders in uniforms with little skirts and gold and black pom poms:

'Give me an A! Give me a C!'

They were gorgeous! They all jumped up at the same time. They wiggled at the same time. It was like being in America. They didn't look scary like our girls.

They could even spell ACADEMY. I thought it had three As but Sir said they were right.

We play in the Under-13 league, but their footballers were HUGE - picked from a special

Academy race of giants. They probably grew them in their brand-new science labs. There were probably rows of big jars where they grew cheerleaders, huge footballers and kids who passed exams.

Maybe that was where all their teachers came from, too ...

The first half

We didn't do too badly in the first half, due to Super Dean. He was everywhere. He was captain and he ran his legs off, saving goals, shooting at the other end, yelling at people. He was a blur.

Sir and I shouted ourselves silly. They scored just before half-time. Their striker put a screamer in the top left of our net from way out. I thought Dean was going to cry when the score went up on the big display board in lights.

| The Academy | 1 | Coalpits High School | 0 |

At half time, though, he was going on to his team:

'We can do this! We've just got to pin

them down. We can score two! Easy!'

Everyone looked at him as if he were nuts.

Sir said:

> 'Dean puts everything into winning, Pig. Do
> you get it now?'

I did. It made me think a bit about the other
two arguments I'd had.

Did Suki really like Kim? I mean, REALLY like him? What was Mum on about? I had to think a bit about how other people felt. It gave me a bit of a headache. I'm rubbish at that stuff. I'm a bloke.

I went back to thinking about the match.

The second half

Just after the start of the second half, Stevie got up off the bench. He said that he felt a bit ill. Then a huge river of sick left his mouth. He was sicker than anyone I've ever seen be sick.

Even when people explode in hospital programmes

on TV, they get nowhere near the giant flood of puke that Steve threw up. It was mainly browny-green, with orange bits. Why are there always orange bits in sick?

He told us afterwards he'd had curry for lunch. The food hadn't changed much really when it came back out. I don't think Stevie's stomach can be working properly, if it goes in and then comes out just the same.

The noise was quite amazing, too. Sort of:

'Huuuuaaaaaarggggghhhhhhh!'

It carried on, as well:

'Huuaaarrrggghhhhhh! Huuaarrggghhhhhhhh!'

The match stopped and the players all came over to watch, as Sir and I leapt out of the way.

Then Stevie went quiet. We all thought he had finished. Silence.

'Huuuuuuuuuuuuuuuuaaaaaaaarrrrrrggggggh-hhhhhhhhhhhh!'

He started up again. This time it actually came out of his nose as well! Out of his nose! It was awesome! If he'd had any more sick left, I think it would have come out of his ears.

All the cheerleaders did silly, girly screaming. Obviously they didn't have a proper chant for being sick. But they were really good. They made up a new chant, straight away:

'Give me a P! Give me a U! Give me a K! Give me an E! What have we got ... ?'

Everyone looked at Stevie. Except Mick Turay, our
striker, who quietly dribbled the ball up to the
other end of the field and into the Academy's
empty goal. Nobody noticed. He even had to
point it out to the ref.

Five minutes before the whistle and it was still
one all.

| The Academy | 1 | Coalpits High School | 1 |

We were too tired to break away and they
were in our half all the time.

Finally their big striker made a break. He was
into the penalty area and our goalie, Jay, came

right out to meet him.

Dean might have barged into their striker on
purpose, or he might have been so tired he fell
into him. Anyway, he brought the striker down.

'No!' Sir shouted, 'No! No! No!

Noooooooooooooooooooooooooo!'

It was a penalty. Jay stomped back to the goal.
The cheerleaders started their routine, shaking
their pom poms and wiggling about. Jay turned
round a bit to watch them.

Jay has problems doing two things at once.
Sometimes he struggles to do one. So I wasn't

surprised when he walked straight into his own

goalpost. Whump! He almost knocked himself out.

The ref wouldn't let him go back on. We had no

goalie to save the penalty.

My bit

I had to change under Sir's coat and go into

goal. My kit was huge and the shorts came down

past my knees. I stood on the goal line. All eyes

were on me. I could feel them. (OK, I couldn't really.)

The cheerleaders were looking at me. I felt myself go red. I had no idea what to do, but I wanted to try my hardest. I couldn't let them down.

Their player stepped back from the ball. I had seen goalies on TV jumping up and down along the goal line before a penalty. So I started to do that. I jumped along the line and waved my arms about like a looney.

Their player started his run up. Just as he kicked
the ball, my huge shorts fell down.

I was wearing special
Christmas pants
underneath: a huge
reindeer head on
a bright green
background. I had

just grown into them.
They were quite a sight. Mum said you could see
them from space.

Their player totally mishit the kick and missed the
goal. He nearly missed the pitch, to be honest.
I went a bit mad then. Someone fetched the

ball back from Outer Space and handed it to me. I stepped out of my shorts and kicked the ball to Dean.

Oh no! I could see he was too tired to run at all. So I ran up the pitch in my reindeer pants, shouting:

'To me, Dean, to me!'

He stopped in surprise. Then he passed to me and I started my run, swerving round one player, two players, three – and screaming at the top of my voice.

Sir shouted:

'Go on, Pig! Go on!'

Some of their players just stopped and watched the little ginger kid in the reindeer pants, running and screaming.

Just past the half-way mark I could hear Sir start to roar:

'Shoot, Pig, Shoot! Shoot!'

How did that happen?

I shot for goal as hard as I could. It was nowhere near. I missed completely.

Then it bounced off one of their defenders.
The other defender controlled it and passed it
back to their goalie – who was laughing so hard
at my pants that he totally missed the ball and
it bobbled over into their goal.

At that exact minute the ref blew the whistle
for full time!

We had won! Two – one! It was up in lights. In
your face!

| The Academy | 1 | Coalpits High School | 2 |

I stood in the middle of the pitch in my
reindeer pants, until Dean jumped up to me to

hug me (in a manly way) and knocked me flat on my face.

I got up, holding my hands crossed in front of the reindeer's nose (and in front of my bits, which were very cold).

On the touch line I could see Suki, Kim, Gran

and The Vampire Baby all going wild. Kim was holding The Vampire Baby up in the air and cheering. It was being sick onto his hair.

Gran was waving her walking stick! Mum came running on with my inhaler and hugged me. They had come to see me play! I was forgiven for being hopeless!

I felt I was on top of the world! I was a hero for once!

The cheerleaders went quiet, but my own team was shouting and cheering:

'Give us a P! Give us an I! Give us a GGG!'

'Give us a P! Give us an I! Give us a GGG!'

'Pig! Pig! Pig!'

'Pig! Pig! Pig!'

'Pig! Pig! Pig!'

It was really sick (in more ways than one).

I wished I could make a hologram of the

match, so I could look at it when I feel sad.

I wished ... I wished I could send it to my dad.

How many PIG books have you read?

About the author

Barbara Catchpole was a teacher for thirty years and enjoyed every minute. She has three sons of her own who were always perfectly behaved and never gave her a second of worry.

Barbara also tells lies.